A LITTLE SPOT OF ANGER

Written & Illustrated by Diane Alber

To my children, Ryan and Anna:

Always remember that you have the power to CALM your ANGRY SPOT down to a PEACEFUL SPOT!

This book belongs to:

_____

_____

_____

Hi! I'm a PEACEFUL SPOT! I'm here to help you CALM down an ANGRY SPOT when one shows up!

An ANGRY SPOT is also known as ANGER.
ANGER is one of the many emotions we can
experience every day. Other emotions are
SADNESS and ANXIETY, too!

We all have these emotions inside us.
But we feel the best when we are in our PEACEFUL SPOT.

Sadness   Anger   Anxiety

It's good to have small spots of emotions, but when they get TOO BIG, you don't feel very good.
So I'm here to show you how to CALM your BIG ANGRY SPOTS down to a very PEACEFUL little size! Like ME!

Your **ANGRY SPOT** can show up
when you are feeling frustrated, afraid, or hurt.
When you are CALM, it is easier to manage this strong emotion.

And I know of a special trick to get your
ANGRY SPOT to CALM down! Want to see?

Yes,
PLEASE!

Let me see your hand!
Now imagine four RED SPOTS are on your fingers
and one GREEN SPOT is on your thumb.

Just like this!

Now repeat after me:

Count the SPOTS from one to four.
Tap, tap, tap and tap once more.

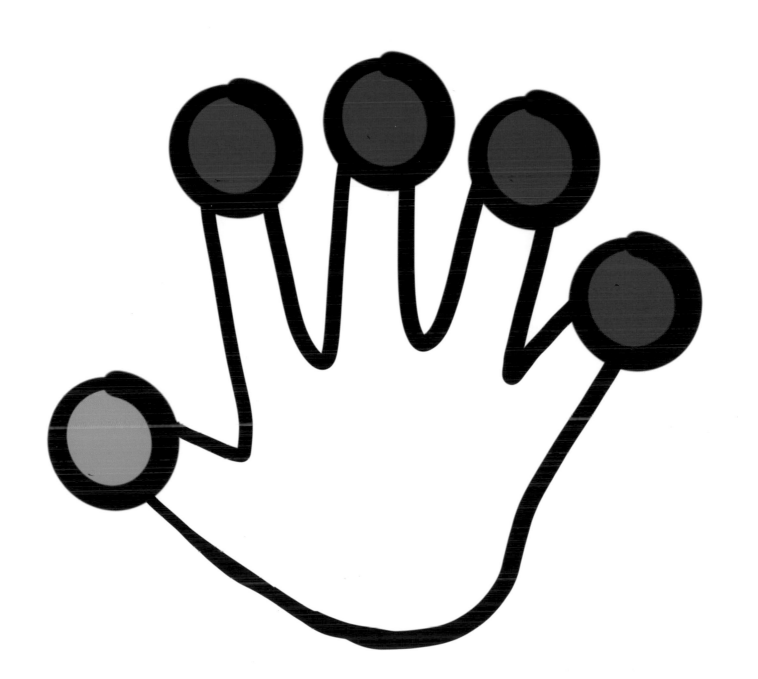

Now fill your lungs
with peaceful air,
and coat your spots
with love and care.

Now that you know what to do. Let's take a look at some situations when your ANGRY SPOT shows up.

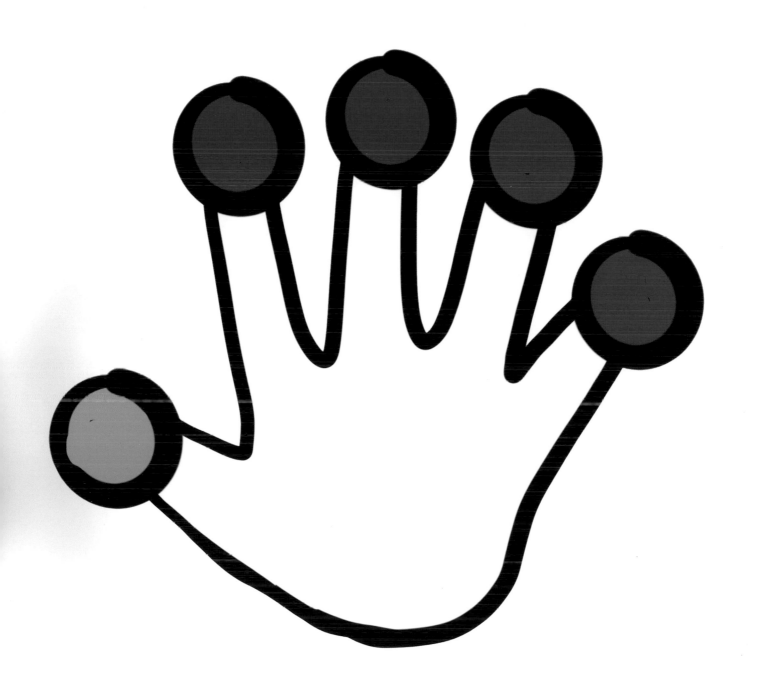

Well, this looks familiar!
Remember when you tried to do something new and it didn't turn out
the way you wanted it to? This can be very frustrating!

Look how big the ANGRY SPOT becomes?

So when you feel like YELLING you should do this trick instead?

AHHHHH!

Exactly! Once you begin counting, you are telling your ANGRY SPOT that it's time to CALM down and get smaller!

Count the SPOTS from one to four.
Tap, tap, tap and tap once more.

Now fill your lungs with peaceful air, and coat your spots with love and care.

Look how the PEACEFUL air really COOLS down an ANGRY SPOT!

I feel so much better!
Everyone has their own style of art, and
I shouldn't compare myself to others.
I'm still learning, and it doesn't
need to be perfect.

I'm so glad I'm
PEACEFUL again!

Oh, dear! Here is another situation where an
ANGRY SPOT gets TOO BIG!

I know when someone takes your toy it can make you
feel AFRAID that you may never see it again.

Instead of STOMPING your feet or GROWLING,
try and CALM your ANGRY SPOT down.
Once you are CALM, you will see that she isn't
trying to be mean, she is just trying to play!

Count the SPOTS from one to four.
Tap, tap, tap and tap once more.

It's working!
The ANGRY SPOT
is already half his size!

Now fill your lungs
with peaceful air,
and coat your spots
with love and care.

When you are CALM, it is easier to
handle ANY situation!

Let's look at some other situations when an ANGRY SPOT shows up.

Like when you feel hurt because you think you have lost your favorite toy.

WHERE IS MY DINOSAUR?

It's in the toy bin! Your ANGRY SPOT made it harder to find.

Or when you try to make a masterpiece but something spills.

MY PAINTING IS RUINED!

Sometimes your ANGRY SPOT makes it hard
to see the wonderful thing you created!
Once your ANGRY SPOT is CALM, you will see that you actually
made amazing splatter art!

When you are CALM it's easier to look at any situation in a positive way. Remember, YOU have the power to CALM your ANGRY SPOT down and make it into a PEACEFUL SPOT!

Count the SPOTS from one to four.
Tap, tap, tap and tap once more.

Now fill your lungs
with peaceful air,
and coat your spots
with love and care.

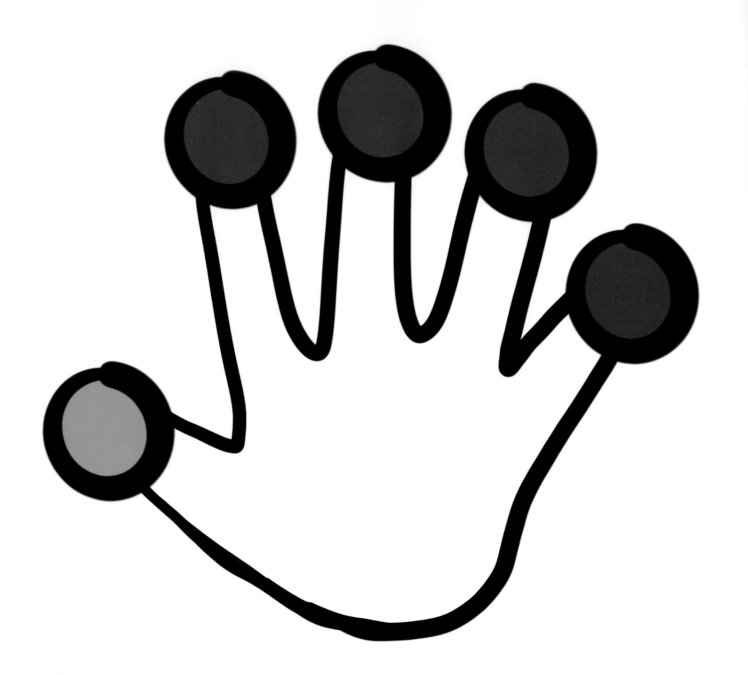

You can imagine your own spots or cut them out of construction paper and tape them to your fingers. You can also get real SPOT stickers in bulk on my website: www.dianealber.com